UGH! A Bug

Mary Bono

Walker & Company

New York

for TANYA

First published in the United States of America in 2002 by
Walker Publishing Company, Inc.

Published simultaneously in Canada by Fitzhenry and Whiteside,
Markham, Ontario L3R 4T8

For information about permission to reproduce selections from
this book, write to Permissions,
Walker & Company, 435 Hudson Street, New York, New York 10014

Library of Congress Cataloging-in-Publication Data

Bono, Mary.
Ugh! a bug / Mary Bono.
p. cm.
Summary: Rhyming text and illustrations present various reactions to
encounters with such bugs as an ant, beetle, and ladybug.
ISBN 0-8027-8799-1 -- ISBN 0-8027-8800-9
[1. Insects--Fiction. 2. Stories in rhyme.] I. Title.

Pz8.3.B635 Ug 2001
[E]--dc21   2001045547

The drawings are colored pencil over watercolor washes;
the bugs are made of plastic clay, with wire legs and acetate wings.

Printed in Hong Kong

2 4 6 8 10 9 7 5 3 1

Ugh!

A bug.

What do you do
when a bug's
bugging you?

*I*f a **FLY**
wouldn't split
when you swatted at it,
would you try to ignore it
or throw a big fit?

Supposing a **S P I D E R**
should slide into view.
Would you scream?
Would you holler?
Just what would you do?
Admire her weaving?
Or think about leaving?

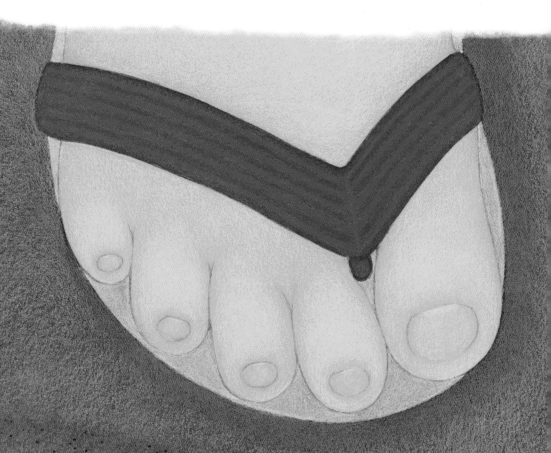

If you spied
a **CENTIPEDE**
slithering by,
would you reach
for a stick?
Run away?
Start to cry?

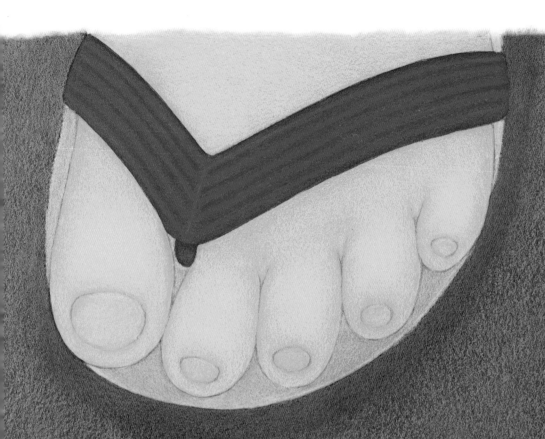

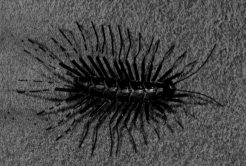

Or see him
home safely
no matter how slow
he step . . .
after step . . .
after step . . .
had to go?

Would you welcome
a wandering **WORM**
to your garden?
What if her wriggling
relatives come?

If an **A N T**
were to ambush
a crumb from
your sandwich,
would you ask him
and all of his friends
in for some?

Would you brake for a **BEETLE** who's blocking your way?

Don't try to hurry him—
he's got all day.

Would you offer a **MOTH**
a nice warm place to linger?

Would you hire an **INCHWORM** to measure your finger?

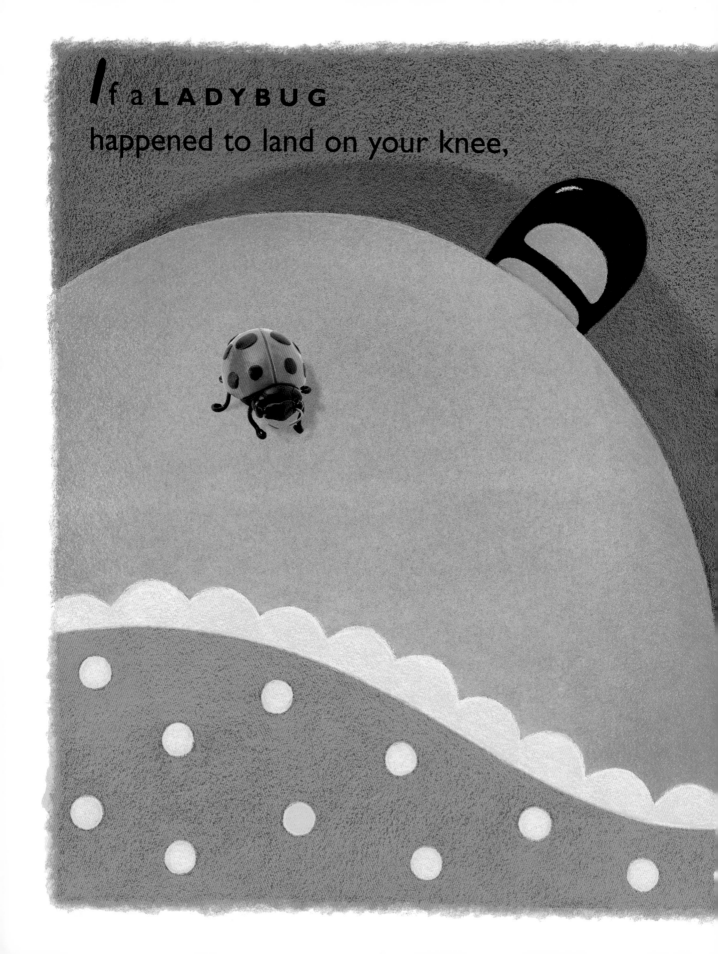

If a **LADYBUG**
happened to land on your knee,

would you greet her politely?
Invite her to tea?

How would you handle
a **F L E A** that keeps flitting
around
and around
and around
where you're sitting?

No!

Flee from him?
Flatten him?
Shout at him,
"No!!!"?
What if you simply
suggest that he go?

Is that a big
B U M B L E B E E
coming toward you?
Don't go ballistic
whatever you do.

Seeing that stinger
might cause you dismay,
but if you'll be cool
she'll buzz out
of your way.

Do **DRAGONFLIES**
suddenly swoop
down and hover?

They're just being nosy
so don't run for cover.

But if a **MOSQUITO**
should head for your hair,
don't think it over—
just get out of there!

There are millions and zillions
of bugs—it is true,
and sometimes it seems like
they're all over you!

Yes—some bugs *are* nasty,
but most bugs are not.
It's really a matter
of which bug you've got.

THE CREEPY,
CRAWLY
CATERPILLAR

Whether hairy or scary
mild-mannered or mean,
pretty or ugly or
somewhere between . . .

spiny or shiny
or speedy
or slow,
there will always
be *some* bugs
wherever you go.

When you're playing outdoors
and you come face to face
with a bug,
just remember
that you're in *her* space!

So next time you see a bug
don't make a fuss—
after all,
there's a lot more of them
than of us.

And please don't forget that
whoever they are—
bugs are happier when
they are not in a jar.

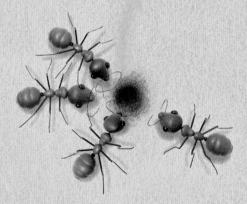